Ruckus

Ruckus

Laurie Elmquist

Illustrated by David Parkins

ORCA BOOK PUBLISHERS

Library and Archives Canada Cataloguing in Publication

Title: Ruckus / Laurie Elmquist; illustrated by David Parkins.
Names: Elmquist, Laurie, author. | Parkins, David, illustrator.
Series: Orca echoes.

Description: Series statement: Orca echoes

Identifiers: Canadiana (print) 20190070633 | Canadiana (ebook) 20190070641 |
ISBN 9781459817951 (softcover) | ISBN 9781459817968 (PDF) |
ISBN 9781459817975 (EPUB)

Classification: LCC PS8609.L574 R83 2019 | DDC jC813/.6—dc23

Library of Congress Control Number: 2019934048
Simultaneously published in Canada and the United States in 2019

*Orca Book Publishers is committed to reducing the consumption of
nonrenewable resources in the making of our books. We make every
effort to use materials that support a sustainable future.*

Summary: In this illustrated early chapter book, a young boy learns to take care
of his newly adopted dog while coping with his parents' separation.

Orca Book Publishers gratefully acknowledges the support for its publishing
programs provided by the following agencies: the Government of Canada,
the Canada Council for the Arts and the Province of British Columbia through
the BC Arts Council and the Book Publishing Tax Credit.

Edited by Liz Kemp
Cover artwork and interior illustrations by David Parkins
Author photo by Ryan Rock

ORCA BOOK PUBLISHERS
orcabook.com

Printed and bound in Canada.

22 21 20 19 • 4 3 2 1

To my brother, Ernie, who loves dogs
as much as I do.

Chapter One

He was a round white lump with black spots and a tail that thumped my face. The first week we got him, Mom wanted to give him back. His mouth was always open, and he had razor-sharp teeth.

"But we just got him," I told her.

"I think he's defective," she said. "He bites everything. All the time. He bites me. He bites you. Everywhere he goes, he causes a ruckus."

The name stuck. *Ruckus.*

We didn't get rid of him that first week, because even Mom had to admit that he was only a puppy and he'd probably grow out of the biting. Now he's older, and he doesn't bite quite as much, although Mom still has to stand in the bathtub when she pulls on her tights. And he still snaps at them like an alligator. But that's what Jack Russells are all about. They were bred to chase rats. Or anything that moves like a rat.

I pick him up and put him in his pen. It's in the corner of the kitchen because he likes to be part of the action.

Mom is getting the house ready for a work meeting with her team. Hazel and I groan. We don't like it when they take over the house. But Mom says it's important for them to get together to strategize.

Recycling is the final frontier. That's what Dad used to say. He says Mom is on a mission to boldly go where no one has gone before, to put a worm composter in every house. She's even trying to get people to grow veggies on their boulevards. Reduce, reuse, recycle.

Dad lives in Vancouver now, in a condo. He says he doesn't have a worm composter. He's not home enough. He has to be away fighting forest fires a lot. Mom and Dad are separated. Hazel says that he used to tease Mom. It was one of their "problems." I just wish they'd figure it out and get back together.

Mom slaps another sticky note on the kitchen cupboard.

"Why does that one say *PARKING LOT*?" I ask.

"That's where we park our ideas," she says.

"I have an idea," says Hazel.

"Write it on a note," says Mom.

TATTOO, writes Hazel, adding a pink sticky note.

"You're thirteen. Too young for a tattoo," says Mom. "It's not even legal to get one before you're eighteen."

"What about a henna tattoo?" she asks. "There's a girl at my school who does them."

Mom goes to the cupboard and moves the pink sticky note to another cupboard that says *LONG-TERM GOALS*.

My sister's face crumples.

"Don't worry," I tell her. "That's where Ruckus used to be. He used to be a *MAYBE*, and now he's here."

Everyone stares at him. He's chewing the eyeball off his stuffed tick. He's got the furry brown body in his teeth, and he's ripping into it.

Mom raises her eyebrow. "A tattoo might have been easier than living with a *Tyrannosaurus rex*."

"Way easier," says Hazel.

I grab the eyeball out of Ruckus's mouth before he swallows it. He's not a *Tyrannosaurus rex*. Not really.

"I like you," I say, leaning down and feeling his whiskery face against mine. He has a soft tongue. He smells good too. He smells like an old sweater that hasn't been washed in a long time.

The doorbell rings, and Ruckus jumps up and barks his head off. That's Mom's team arriving. I'm on duty. I have to take him far, far away from here. Hazel and I are going to Gonzo Beach, where he can run off leash. Dogs have the IQ of two-year-olds, but I'm pretty sure Ruckus is a genius. I wave the leash at him, and he knows where we're going without me even saying anything.

Chapter Two

Today the beach is full of dogs, sniffing each other's butts and chasing each other. Lots of teenagers too. Hazel lays out her blanket and slides on her sunglasses like a movie star.

It's September, but it's one of those hot ones that still feels like summer. A huge, shaggy dog walks up to Ruckus and sniffs. Ruckus sits his butt down in the sand. That's his way of saying, *Okay, Big Guy. You're the boss.*

"What is he?" I ask a man with a scruffy beard and dreadlocks.

"Labradoodle," he says. "His name's Yankee."

"Yankee Doodle."

"You got it," he says.

Ruckus starts to wiggle and pounce, and then he takes off in the sand. He runs around and around with the big Yankee Doodle chasing him. He zigs and zags.

"That's some dog you've got," says the man.

A curly-haired boy comes up to him and holds up his arms. He looks about two years old. Still has the big diaper under his pants. The man scoops him up and puts him on his shoulders. The kid grabs onto the guy's hair with a toothy smile.

Ruckus is standing at the water, his tongue hanging out of his mouth.

"I'd better go," I say. "He looks kind of tired now."

"Yeah," says the man. "See you later."

I grab Ruckus's harness. When I look up the man is walking along the beach, the kid's head bobbing up and down. That's a lucky kid. Going to the beach with his dad and his dog. I wish my dad was here. A knot the size of a refrigerator hardens in my chest.

Vancouver is a two-hour ferry ride away. It sucks to have an ocean between us. In that ocean are whales and seals and salmon. Sometimes I wish I were a seal and could swim to Dad. When I tell my sister Hazel, she says I'd need to be an eagle too. That way I could fly once I reached the land. I could fly to Dad's condo. Or, better yet, I could fly to the forest fires that Dad is working on.

I wander along the beach to a rocky outcropping. It's full of tidal pools. I lean down and poke a sea urchin. The sound of the ocean is louder out here. The waves roll against the rocks, tumbling the seaweed in and out. I keep Ruckus on his leash. I don't want him jumping after the birds or falling into the water. It's too deep. And really cold. Dad used to say, *Never turn your back on the ocean. Rogue waves can sweep you right off a rock.* I don't want a rogue wave to get Ruckus.

Dad taught me a lot of things about the ocean and the forest. He wasn't always a firefighter. He used to plant trees, but it wasn't steady work, and Mom said it wasn't enough for a growing family. That's when he got into fighting forest fires, but then he was away a lot.

Not just in British Columbia but other provinces too. Sometimes even Washington or Oregon.

Somewhere in there, the fighting started between him and Mom. It was the silent type of fighting. Mom heading to work without giving Dad a kiss goodbye like she always used to. Dad staying out late at night even when he was home from a fire. Dad sleeping on the couch. The day he left for Vancouver, he put everything he could into his truck. His surfboards were in the back. His duffel bags bulged with clothes and boots. He put his guitar on the front seat.

Mom stood in the doorway, her shoulders stiff. I wished she would run to the truck and tell him to come back.

I did.

I ran to the window. "Dad, don't forget us," I told him.

"Are you kidding?" he said. "I'm going to text you when I get to the ferry."

"Like you always do."

Mom had given me a phone when I turned nine so I could talk to Dad when he was out of town.

"Uh-huh," he said, "like always."

"Bye, Hazelnut," he called to my sister.

"Bye, Dad," she said, not moving from Mom's side. Her hands were crossed over her chest.

"I love you guys," Dad called as he drove away.

I hate love sometimes because it makes me feel sick, like I just got punched in the stomach. That's the way it was when Dad left eight months ago. I still get anxious sometimes. It makes me fidgety. I try not to let Mom see, because she's trying to act like everything is normal. I am too.

"Reece," calls Hazel.

I look up.

"I've been trying to get your attention." She climbs up on the rock in her bare feet. "Time to go home."

"Uh-huh," I say.

"What are you doing?" she asks.

"Looking at hermit crabs," I say, pointing to the pool, where crabs are scuttling under the weight of their borrowed shells.

"Oh," she says.

"Yeah, it's for science," I tell her. "Mr. Sharman wants us to do some kind of report on the intertidal zone."

I'm not sure she believes me, because she's known me all my life. But I don't want her saying I'm too broody or telling Mom I'm not happy or something. I don't want Mom getting that big crease in her forehead and making me drink more kale smoothies. Or suggesting I call Dad. I'll call Dad when I'm ready.

Chapter Three

When Mom gets up in the morning her diamond earrings are missing. "I put them right here," she says, pointing to the bedside table.

"Maybe you only thought you did," I say.

"I remember putting them here," she says, "and wondering if they would be safe."

Ruckus has already chewed and swallowed one of the eyeballs off his tick and the antlers off his moose. But they were soft and covered in slobber. Earrings are hard and pointy.

I get this awful sinking feeling inside my stomach.

"He looks guilty," says Hazel.

Mom frowns. "I have my big presentation today. I don't have time to take him to the vet."

"Will they pump out his stomach?" I ask.

"I don't know what they'll do," she says. "Maybe an X-ray? It will cost a fortune."

Ruckus runs out of the room and comes back with his ball. He drops it at my feet. "Do you have diamonds in your belly?" I ask him.

He nudges the ball and barks.

I whip it down the hall.

Mom looks at her watch and groans. "We're going to be late," she says.

"I'll stay home with him," I offer.

"No," she says.

"Maybe he just knocked them off the table," Hazel suggests. We get down on our hands and knees and look everywhere. Under the table. Under the bed.

Mom runs her hands over the carpet. "Nothing," she says. "And now we're really late."

"What are we going to do?" I ask.

"Put him in his crate," she says. "I'll take him to work."

"Really?" I ask.

"It's all we can do," she says. "That way I can keep an eye on him at least." She doesn't look happy. She looks like she wishes she'd never got me a dog.

* * *

When I get home from school I call Dad. I haven't talked to him in a while. I guess I've been mad at him. Just a little. I know he's been away working all summer, but still. He's my dad and he should be around more. What good is a dad if he's far away?

"What happened?" he asks.

"He ate Mom's diamond earrings," I say.

I can hear him laughing. He has a deep laugh that sounds like a rumble.

"It's not funny," I tell him.

"The ones I bought her?" he asks.

"I guess so," I say.

"Well, the good news is that they were pretty small," he says. "I couldn't afford big ones."

"You think he'll be okay?" I ask.

"It's like that marble you ate," he says. "You were just a baby, and I thought your mother was going to have a fit. In the end, it came out in your poop. Really pretty little thing. Blue, as I recall."

"So the earrings will come out?"

"Yes, 100 percent sure. What goes in must come out."

I breathe a big sigh of relief. I'm glad I called Dad. It feels good to hear him laugh. It feels like maybe things aren't so bad. It's okay if Ruckus eats a few things. It's what puppies do.

"You coming to visit soon?" I ask.

"A couple more weeks," he says.

"Okay," I say.

* * *

It's my job to go through Ruckus's poop. Mom decided not to take him to the vet because he didn't seem sick. When she got home from work, she let him out of his crate. "He was his same boisterous self," she says.

I walk him around the block, and when he does his business, I gather it up in a bag as usual. But I don't throw it away. I take it home with me. I dump the poop into a sieve and put the hose on it. You'd be surprised what's in there. Pieces of bark, tiny pebbles from the beach, undigested rawhide bone.

"Anything good?" Hazel calls from the porch.

"No," I say.

The next day he poops twice, and I do the same thing. I dump it in the sieve like I'm mining for gold. I get some strange looks from people walking by the driveway. One workman asks me if I lost

something. *Duh. Well, obviously I've lost something.*

But still nothing. Maybe Mom's wrong. Maybe she put the earrings somewhere and forgot where she put them. Like that time we went away for a weekend and she hid her best gold bracelet and couldn't find it for six months. Then she found it in her ribbon box. Maybe she did something like that again.

"No," she says. "I'm absolutely positive I left them on my night table."

So maybe they're jabbing into Ruckus's belly. Poking into his stomach. Stuck there like porcupine quills.

"Maybe he needs an X-ray," I tell Hazel.

"That's going to cost a lot of money," she says, worried. "I'm not sure Mom has it."

"She could ask Dad for it," I say.

"Dad just sent us money for school clothes," she says.

Ruckus nuzzles my hand, and I scratch his chin. He looks at me with those chocolate eyes and I feel my insides go all squishy. If something happened to him, I don't know what I'd do. He feels like a part of me. If only he didn't eat everything his nose comes in contact with.

Chapter Four

"You could always crowdsource," says my friend Aaron. He's wearing his sleek gray housecoat over jeans and a white T-shirt. Very James Bond. He has a few different housecoats that he wears to school.

"What's crowdsourcing?" I ask as we do our math problems. Aaron sits in my pod. We are the Sharks.

"You go online and ask for money," he says.

"And people give it to you?" I ask.

"My brother's class got money for their playground equipment," he says. "You could probably get enough for an X-ray."

"I don't know if my mom would let me," I say. "She's always saying we have to earn money if we want it."

"Very old-fashioned," says Aaron.

"Maybe we could set up a stand and sell stuff?"

"Like what?"

"I could draw pictures of Ruckus," I say.

"Sure," he says. "Or we could make a *Save Ruckus* bumper sticker."

* * *

That night I call Dad. Again. It's good to hear his voice. He's putting bandages on his blisters. Says they are as big as cucumbers. New boots. They're biting at the top of his ankle.

"How's that dog of yours? Anything show up?" he asks.

"Nothing yet," I say.

"He's a dog," he tells me. "They're tough."

"He's little," I say.

"You got any sardines in the cupboard?"

"I don't know."

"Look way in the back of the pantry. Your mom hates 'em, but I love them, so there's probably a can or two still buried back there. Put some on his food. It will loosen him up. If the earrings are in there, they'll pop out."

"Poop out," I say.

He laughs. "Guaranteed. Next time we talk, your mom's going to be wearing them in her ears."

"Ugh," I say.

"Tell her to clean them with hydrogen peroxide. Good as new."

I want to tell Dad how much I love him, but it feels weird saying it over the phone, so I just grunt.

"And buddy, call me if they don't come out tomorrow. We'll go to plan B."

"What's plan B?"

"X-ray, surgery, whatever it takes. Tell your ma to call me."

"Thanks, Dad." He gets it. He gets that Ruckus is counting on us to figure things out. Even if it means going to the vet.

"Bye, Dad," I say.

After I finish talking to him, I pull out my homework. Ruckus jumps on me and licks my face so hard I can't breathe. He gets his tongue right inside my nose, like he's trying to reach my brain. He's been chewing his pig's ear.

"Okay, Smelly Breath," I tell him. "Okay, okay."

* * *

In bed, I can hear Mom on the phone. Her voice comes up through a vent in my floor. She's asking Dad for money. I can tell because her voice gets louder, and she sounds really serious. Last month it was for school supplies, and the month before it was for Hazel's braces.

My sister has a lot of big teeth in her head, and she had to have some of them removed so the front ones could be pulled back. She looks less like a gopher now, but her teeth are still big. She says big teeth are more attractive than tiny teeth. Hollywood stars have big chompers. "You'll need braces too," she said.

"Will not," I said.

"Whatever," she said, which means she thinks she's right but can't be bothered to talk to me anymore.

I push my front teeth back with my thumb. Maybe I can save Dad some money and just push them back every night. That way we could take the money and spend it on Ruckus. Maybe we should have some kind of SAVE RUCKUS fund because he does stupid things like eat things he shouldn't.

I hear Mom's voice getting louder and louder. "The dog was your idea, and now I have to find a way to pay for him."

I don't hear what Dad says, but I wish he could talk to Mom like he does to me. I wish he could explain things and make her happy.

Hazel said I shouldn't get my hopes up. She said Dad and Mom will not be getting back together, because Dad is too immature. He hasn't figured out what he wants in life.

"But he makes her laugh sometimes," I said.

"He makes everyone laugh, not just Mom."

She said it like it was a bad thing, and I haven't figured out why. Making people laugh is a good thing. That's why I make comics and tell jokes at school. It always makes everything better. If I don't know the answer to something, sometimes I can get away with a joke. Then I bounce the question over to Aaron, my best friend. He usually knows the answer.

I listen hard. Mom's voice is getting loud again. Then silence, like she's off the phone.

I pet Ruckus. He's curled against my stomach under the covers. He's warm and soft. Holding onto him makes me less anxious. I can feel his hot breath on my hands. Do parents ever get back together? Everyone says it never happens.

Chapter Five

In the morning I stand outside on the curb and wait for Ruckus to do his business. He's sniffing the grass. He's circling around. Then he stops and sits. He stares across the road at another dog.

"We have to go," says Mom.

"He hasn't done anything yet," I say. "We have to wait for the sardines to kick in."

Our neighbor is putting out his recycling. Ruckus watches him. He woofs low at the back of his throat. Mom doesn't like it when he barks, so now he fake-barks. A quiet *whoof, whoof, whoof.*

Mom opens the door of the Volkswagen bus and climbs in. She starts the engine, and a puff of smoke pops out the muffler. "Come on," she says. "There's no more time."

I slide the door open and load Ruckus into his crate. Hazel piles the posters in beside me and jumps into the passenger seat. We are going to Mom's big march on the Legislature. It's an important building in Victoria where the government meets. It's also where people demonstrate about things they believe in.

Mom's been working on her speech for months. She wants big companies to reduce their packaging. She says it's up to us consumers to put our money where it will do the most good. No plastic containers. She wants everyone to think about growing their own vegetables. Yank up the grass and plant your salad greens. But where are all the dogs going to pee if we yank up the grass?

Ruckus whines in his crate. He doesn't care about recycling. He'd rather be at the beach. I feel that way too, but I can't say anything or Hazel will glare at me and call me selfish. She says it's important to support Mom because of all the things she does for us.

I don't know why the sardines didn't work. Maybe Dad was wrong, and the earrings are never going to come out on their own. We pull into a parking spot. Mom glances back at Ruckus. "I'm not happy about bringing him, but it's just for an hour or two."

"I've got him," I say.

Hazel and Mom unload the posters. A bunch of people come over to help. It's Mom's team. They're all wearing T-shirts with a vegetable garden on the front. On the back the T-shirts say, *They paved paradise and put up a parking lot, so we're fighting back with urban gardens.*

"Kind of wordy," I say.

"Can't say everything in two words," says Mom.

The Legislature sits up on a hill with a big green lawn in front of it. There are lots of people wearing sun hats and carrying posters. There's even a giant Poop walking around. It's a guy in a brown costume. He is protesting the pollution of the ocean. Some cities dump raw sewage straight into the harbor. A lot of people think it's wrong.

Ruckus is pulling on his leash, looking at the giant Poop. Maybe he thinks it's some kind of big wiener dog or something. I try to get him under control, but he's jumping and biting my hands. He wants to go over to where the giant Poop is standing. Right in the middle of the grass.

"Okay, okay," I say, giving in.

His tail is wagging, and he lunges across the lawn. In a few seconds we're at the giant Poop's side. He's handing out pamphlets, and he gives me one. Ruckus sniffs at Poop's sneakers. Then he starts to sniff at the grass. Then he starts to circle around, his butt low to the ground.

Surrounded by people and right at the feet of the giant Poop, Ruckus squats.

And poops. It is a giant poop. It smells terrible, and it squirts, and everyone takes a giant step backward. Even the giant Poop, who holds his hands up to his fake nose.

My face turns beet red. I wish a giant spaceship would show up right about now and beam me up. I look around for Mom and Hazel, but they are too far away to help. There's only one thing to do. I get out my bag. I scoop it up, yanking up a handful of grass with it. I twirl the bag around and knot it.

Then I squish it, feeling for the earrings.

As a small crowd watches, I squish, squish, squish. Then I feel something. Something small and hard. Rock hard. I follow the rock-hard thing down a slender stick to the part at the end that holds the earring on. "They're in here!" I hold up the poop in triumph.

Everyone stares at me like I'm crazy, but I don't care. Ruckus and I are running. An all-out sprint across the big green lawn, the poop bag bouncing against my leg. We have to find Mom and tell her.

I run toward her, waving the bag. She's just about to climb the podium to make her speech. She cups her hand to her ear.

"Mom, I found your earrings!" I yell.

She taps the microphone. "Can everyone hear me?"

I thrust the bag into her hands. "They're right here," I say. "Your earrings. I feel them."

She looks out over the crowd, "It seems my son has recovered my earrings, which the dog ate." She hands me back the bag and whispers, "Good job."

The crowd laughs.

"Now, with that business attended to, shall we move on?" she asks, her voice echoing across the lawn.

Ruckus pulls me away. He doesn't like crowds. He'd rather be sitting under a big tree and waiting for Mom. Me too. Plus, I'm carrying the bag. And it's still kind of smelly. Luckily, I have my backpack, and I put the bag in there for safekeeping.

Sardines. Dad was right. Ruckus crawls onto my lap and closes his eyes. It's been a big day for him. It's not every day he poops diamonds. Or protests at the Legislature.

Chapter Six

Dad is here. He arrived late last night. I found him on the couch when I woke up, his big toes sticking up from the blanket. Ruckus looks at the lump on the couch and starts barking.

"Shhh, it's Dad," I tell him.

Dad stirs, and his voice rumbles out from under the covers. "Is that him? The terror? You going to give your old man a hug or what?"

I jump on him. Ruckus does too. He's snapping and lunging at Dad's hands. He's licking my chin, then Dad's. "Don't bite," I say. "Don't bite."

Dad holds him up in the air so he can't do anything. Ruckus shows his *Tyrannosaurus rex* teeth and growls.

"You pipsqueak," he says. "What do you weigh? Fifteen pounds? I got a thigh that weighs more than you."

Ruckus cocks his head like he's listening. He stops wriggling. I think he knows Dad's the Big Dog. Dad kind of looks like a big dog, too. His hair is long. He's got a beard.

"I'm going to grow my hair long like yours," I say.

"Better check with your ma first," he says, setting Ruckus down on the floor. "She might have something to say about it."

He squeezes me in one of his bear hugs, so hard I think my ribs are going to break, but it's a good feeling, like my head is going to pop off with happiness.

"What are we doing today?" he asks.

Dad and I are early birds. We get up before Mom and Hazel, which is a good thing, because Hazel will drag Dad shopping as soon as she sees him.

"I didn't know you were coming," I say. "Why didn't you tell me?"

"Told you I was coming *soon*," he says, raking his hair with his hands.

"Yeah," I say. "You did."

"So let me wash up a bit and what? We'll hit the beach? I'll grab my guitar. Maybe you can get us something to eat, put it in a sack."

"We have to take Ruckus," I say. "It's my job in the morning to walk him."

"Oh yeah," he says. "Bring the dog along. Maybe he can go for a swim or something."

"He doesn't swim yet," I yell after him. "The waves are pretty big down there."

Dad's singing in the washroom. He splashes around in the bathroom like a sea lion. Mom is a lot quieter. I never noticed that before. Dad brings a lot of noise with him.

* * *

You'd think otters wouldn't stink so bad. They swim in the ocean. Their brown fur is sleek and shiny. But their dens stink. "Ruckus!" I yell. "Get out of there."

The den is on the beach, but higher up in the grass. Ruckus is rolling his nose in crab shells. Then his body. He's pushing himself sideways along the grass. I grab him and hook him on his leash. I know we're in trouble.

"We have to go home," I tell Dad.

"But we just got here," he says. "What about our breakfast?" He holds up the bag of bagels. His guitar is slung over his shoulder.

"He stinks like a dead rat," I tell him.

"Put him in the ocean."

I take Ruckus down to the water and throw a stick. He dives in. He coughs and splutters. He goes in deeper than he's ever gone before. He stretches his little skinny neck out to the stick. He's not afraid of anything. But I don't want him to go too far. I wade in and nab the stick before it floats out of reach. I throw it toward the shore.

"How does he smell now?" asks Dad.

"Like a rotting corpse," I say.

"But better, right?" Dad strums a chord. I lay with my back to a log, feeling the sun on my face. I don't want to leave either. As long as Ruckus isn't bothering anybody, it's okay. Not like there's tons of people down here right now. Just the usual dog walkers. Dad bends over his guitar, the chords sounding sweet and easy.

A group of women stands in a circle on the beach with their dogs. One of them has a big dog, a Rhodesian ridgeback. Ruckus likes big dogs. I see his ears perk up. I whistle for him, but it's too late. He's already made a beeline for it.

Dad doesn't care. He keeps playing, and it makes me not care either. Ruckus jumps around the ridgeback, and they chase each other in circles. The lady walks toward us. She's wearing a jean jacket and flowery tights. Her reddish-brown hair shines in the sunlight.

"You boys are up early," she says.

She usually sees me around this time, so I'm not sure why this morning is any different, but she's not really looking at me. She's looking at Dad.

He nods and smiles but goes on playing.

Ruckus runs at our feet, jumping on the lady. She's got treats in her pocket, and she brings one out for him. "Oh, that's horrible," she says, wrinkling her nose. "He's rolled in something."

"Yup," I say. "He stinks."

She backs up and keeps on backing up. I don't mind. I don't mind when she leashes her dog and drags it to the opposite end of the beach. I like it when it's just Dad and me. He starts into a new song, and this time he sings the words. I sit beside him, singing them too.

At first I don't notice that Ruckus is gone. He just slipped away. It must have been when Dad was showing me how to make the chord. *Press this string with the baby finger, this one with the next two fingers.* It was hard to keep the strings from buzzing.

I shield my eyes against the sun. "Dad, where's Ruckus?" I ask.

He looks around. "Can't see him," he says, putting his guitar over his shoulder. "I suppose that's a bad thing."

"Yup," I say, scanning the houses that stand above the beach. "Could be really bad."

We run along the beach, calling his name and peering into backyards. Some of them are wild and tangled yards behind small wooden fences that would be easy to jump over. Some of them are manicured lawns with sharply trimmed bushes and water fountains. These ones are usually behind wire fences with locked gates. One of these gates is open.

I know the man who lives here. Well, I don't know him, but his name is Mr. McGregor, and he's a creep.

He stands behind his fence and yells down at people to get off his property, even though the beach is not his property. Still, he yells stuff like, "You people don't pay taxes. When you pay my taxes, you can walk on my land."

Hazel once yelled back, "We're kids. Kids don't pay taxes."

But it didn't make any difference.

This morning his yard is quiet. Dad and I take a few steps inside the open gate. My heart is thumping. Maybe Mr. McGregor has the place booby-trapped. Maybe we're going to lose a leg in a bear trap. What if Ruckus is caught in a trap?

"Ruck-us," I call.

"RUCKUS!" Dad yells.

I see something move. A flash of black and white, close to the house. It looks like Ruckus's head. Only there's something weird. Something in his mouth. He's acting really strange, and he's hunkered down. He has something.

"What you got, fella?" asks Dad, creeping up on him.

A window shoots open and Mr. McGregor sticks his head out. "Get off my property! This is private property, and you can't trespass. I'm calling the police."

"Whoa," says Dad, holding out his hand. "We're just getting our dog here. We're not doing any harm."

"You got a dog?" he asks.

I wish I'd told Dad that there's one thing Mr. McGregor hates more than people. Dogs. Especially if they're loose and running on his property.

"Get that dog off my land!" yells Mr. McGregor. His face is red, and the veins in his head are bulging. He's bald.

His head is shaped like a moon, and his face has craters like its surface. When he gets mad he balloons up even more, like all the blood is rushing to his head. One of these days he's going to pop, and there will be brains everywhere.

"Gladly," says Dad. "But it looks like he's got something there."

The window slams shut and a door opens. Mr. McGregor is wearing his pajamas, and he's holding a big fishnet. He's going to throw it over Ruckus like a salmon.

"If that dog has my cat in his mouth, he's dead," says Mr. McGregor, lunging toward Ruckus.

Dad gets to Mr. McGregor before he can strike with his net. He catches his arm and holds it in the air. "Now," he says, "let's just take this one step at a time. I believe our dog has something of yours in its mouth, but it's no cat."

Ruckus is crouched near a cedar hedge. He is hunkered over something furry. Bigger than a mouse, smaller than a cat. I hope it's not a bunny.

"Bring it here," I say, creeping closer.

He picks it up in his mouth and moves backs. He lets out a low growl like he does when he has a sock. But it's no sock.

"Come here, boy," says Dad.

Ruckus backs up even farther.

Mr. McGregor is on his phone. "Accosted in my own yard," he says. "You get a cruiser over here."

I don't know what *accosted* means, but it can't be good.

I circle in behind Ruckus. It worked once when Hazel distracted him with treats.

I motion for Dad to stay out in front. He keeps talking to him nice and low. "Good boy," I hear him saying. "That's a good boy. You got something to show me."

I leap on him and scoop him up. He's got the thing in his mouth, and I see

what it is now. A rat. It's a big dead one, with a long tail.

"Drop it!" I order.

I take him over to the fountain and shake him above it. It works with the bathtub because he's afraid of baths. I dangle him out far from my body. He doesn't like all that air around him.

He drops the rat.

I clip his leash on and hug him tight.

"That dog's a menace," says Mr. McGregor, stomping up to me. He shakes his fist in my face. "He's got no tag. Do you see that? No license."

Dad looks at the guy likes he's crazy. "Take your rat and stick it where the sun don't shine," he says, putting his arm around me. We turn around and walk through the gate, slamming it shut.

The beach feels good under our feet. I let Ruckus down on the sand.

"He really does stink," I say.

From the beach, we hear sirens up on the road. Dad rolls his eyes. "I guess we should go talk to them."

"Are they going to take Ruckus away?" I ask.

He laughs. "For killing a rat? I don't think so."

"For trespassing?"

"You worry too much, buddy," he says. "I got it covered."

"What about Mom?" I whisper.

"Well...that's a different kettle of fish," he says.

* * *

As we walk in the door, Hazel grabs Dad in an enormous hug. "You're here," she says. "Mom said you guys were busted by the cops.

"What's that smell?" She holds her nose, pointing at Ruckus. "OH, THAT'S AWFUL. Why does he stink like a dead fish?" She looks at me like it's my fault.

"Otter poop," I say.

Mom is on the phone. We can hear her voice coming from the kitchen.

"It's him," Hazel whispers. "That's the fifth time he's called."

"Uh-huh," says Mom, walking toward us. "Yes, Mr. McGregor. Thanks for telling me. I'll do something right away. Yes. Yes. I understand."

Mom looks at Dad. "You accosted our neighbor?"

"He didn't do anything," I say.

"The cops were cool," he says. "We worked it out."

She turns to me, her face red. "You're grounded for a month. You will walk to school and home. That's it. After dinner you will walk around the block with Ruckus. You are not going to the beach. You are not ever to step foot on Mr. McGregor's property again."

"Go easy," says Dad.

"Easy?" says Mom. "I'm doing the parenting here. And there's nothing easy about it."

"But Mom," I say.

"No buts," she says. "And what is this about a tag? What happened to Ruckus's tag?"

"I don't know," I say. "Maybe when he got into the otter poop, he lost it."

Hazel is making motions behind Mom's head like I shouldn't say any more, but it's a bit late now.

"Bathe him," Mom says to me. "Get the stink out *or else*."

* * *

Dad stays all day. He takes Hazel out shopping. Then he and Mom spend some time together, just the two of them. They have things to talk about. Then he catches the ferry. At dinner Mom is kind of quiet.

Hazel kicks my foot.

"Sorry, Mom," I say, pushing my corn around my plate. "I'll keep a better eye on Ruckus from now on."

Dad always says there's a point where you should just shut up and say you're sorry. He says even if you have a really good reason for doing what you do, not everyone sees it the same way. Especially Mom. If you see it one way, she's going to see it the opposite.

"Well, we got through it," she says. "That's what's important. We hit these bumps and we plow through."

Hazel and I look at each other.

"Your dad won't be back for a little while," says Mom. "He's going to California for a couple of months. He'd like to try living there now that fire season is over. He's got some friends in the construction business."

My stomach drops. California is even farther away than Vancouver.

"What does he know about construction?" asks Hazel.

"He says he wants to learn." Mom chews slowly, like she needs to grind her meat down to dust.

Dad never said anything about the States. He left it for Mom to tell us. He's going away for a couple of months and he didn't tell us. He does that, I realize. He likes to tell us good stuff, but not the bad stuff.

"I'm not mad at you," says Mom, looking at me. "I just want you to be careful. Keep Ruckus on a leash for a while. A dog is a big responsibility."

I swallow hard. "I know, Mom."

Chapter Seven

Ruckus and I are in the doghouse. All week we've been tiptoeing around Mom. I've been making my bed and picking up my socks. I don't want to be grounded until I'm Hazel's age. Ruckus doesn't want to go back to the breeder's. Which is what happens to dogs that are bad.

Hazel told me that. "You give the dog back to the breeder and they find a new home for him."

"Who gives him back?"

"Well, the family that doesn't want him anymore."

"Who would ever do that?"

I'll die before I let that happen to Ruckus.

I make a list for Mom to remind her of all his good points. I post it on the fridge, so she'll see it first thing.

Fun stuff dogs do

they smile
sneeze in your face
double hiccup (two fast hiccups at a time)
fetch things (sticks, balls, socks and underwear)
sleep on your head
lick your eyeballs

Mom is humming when she walks into the kitchen the next morning. She's wearing jeans rolled up at the bottom and her Vans. She has a T-shirt with a star in the middle. I wait for her to say something about Ruckus, the Jack Russell terror. But...nothing. She goes to the bottom of the stairs and calls for Hazel.

When she comes back she opens the fridge, pausing to read the list. "Hmmm," she says. "How about eggs? I think we all need a good breakfast this morning before we head out."

"Are we going somewhere?" I ask.

"We are," she says. She whips some eggs in a bowl and pours them into a pan.

Hazel throws herself into a seat and helps herself to a big pile of scrambled eggs. "Where?" she asks.

"It's a surprise," says Mom. "It's something I've been thinking about for a while."

Ruckus puts a paw on my knee. He's not supposed to beg at the table, and I push him away. "On your mat," I tell him.

He stares at me.

"Sit," I say.

He stares.

Mom is watching him, one eyebrow arched. Usually she'd put Ruckus in his pen. She'd say something about him never doing what he's told. I look over at Hazel. She's looking at Ruckus too. He nudges my hand for food.

Mom gets up from the table and fills her travel mug with coffee. She grabs her keys. "I'll be out in the bus when you're ready. Oh, and bring Ruckus. He's coming too. We're all going for a ride."

The front door slams. Hazel and I exchange looks.

"What's up?" I ask.

"I don't know. Mom didn't say anything to me." Hazel bites her lip like she doesn't want to tell me something but it's there on the tip of her tongue.

"What?" I ask.

"It's just something she said the other night. She said Ruckus brings a lot of chaos into our lives."

"Bad chaos or good chaos?" I ask.

"Is there a good kind?" my sister asks, scratching her head.

"She'd tell us if she was thinking of giving him back," I say. "She'd call a family meeting. We'd all get a vote."

"We didn't get a vote on Dad and her," Hazel says, her eyes lowered. "We didn't get a vote on Dad going to California."

She has a point. I can't eat anything. I shove the rest of my eggs between two pieces of toast and wrap it all in a napkin. If Ruckus and I have to make a run for it, we might need food. There's no way I'm letting anyone take him from me.

I grab his harness, pull it over his head and snap on his leash. In our VW bus I put him in his crate. On the seat beside me is his duffel bag. In it are all his toys—his stuffed tick, orange ball, ropey tug thing, bunny without any stuffing.

If all his stuff is here, Mom must be taking him back.

She turns on the ignition and adjusts the rearview mirror. "Everyone set?"

I get a lump in my throat the size of Jupiter. I grab the seat belt and jam the ends together. I swipe the tears from my eyes. I have a whole car ride to talk her out of it.

"Ruckus has been really good all morning," I say. "He ate all his food. And he peed. He pooped too."

"Good," she says, pulling the Volkswagen away from the curb.

"Where did you say we were going?" asks Hazel. She always twists her long hair to one side when she's anxious. She's doing it now.

"Saanich," Mom says.

"Where you got Ruckus?" I ask.

"Shhh, no more questions," says Mom.

She speeds past the mall and out of the city. The VW makes a chugging sound as she gets its speed up to eighty kilometers an hour. She clicks on the radio and hums along. She turns off the highway and onto a road that winds through farmland. We pass a sign that says *Organic Eggs $4*.

"On the way back I'll get some of those," she says.

Eggs. How can she think of eggs at a time like this?

I poke my fingers through Ruckus's crate. His teeth chew the ends of my fingers, but not hard. "You're a good dog," I tell him, loud enough for Mom to hear. "You know how to fetch. You're friendly with other dogs. You don't smell. You like everybody. You're smart."

Mom looks at me in the rearview mirror. "I hope he's smart."

She's slowing down. She's pulling into a farm. Horses graze in the front field. There's a barn and a gravel parking lot.

There's a gate, and behind the gate are Jack Russells, about five of them, all jumping and barking.

"Where are we?" I ask.

"This is where I got Ruckus," Mom says. "This is the breeder's."

"NO!" I yell, throwing my arms around Ruckus's crate.

Mom spins around, her eyes startled.

"WE AREN'T GIVING HIM BACK," I shout. My eyes start to sting, and I can't breathe.

"Who said anything about giving him back?" says Mom.

"Isn't that what you want to do?" I say, wiping my nose. "Give him back?"

"No," she says. "This is a class for dogs. It's called an agility class. The breeder thought it would help Ruckus focus his energy."

I swallow hard.

"It's a good surprise," says Hazel. "Isn't it, Reece?"

"Yeah," I say, barely breathing.

"It's where they go through tunnels and over jumps," says Mom, her voice gentle. "It's supposed to be really fun."

She flings open the door, and she and Hazel climb out. The breeder walks up to the VW and shakes Mom's hand.

I open the crate, grab hold of Ruckus and squeeze him. "Looks like you're going to school."

When I get out of the van, I'm smiling like a goof. I try to get my face to go normal, but it keeps on smiling. All around me, cars are pulling into the lot. Dogs are straining on their leashes or jumping on their owners. Wild, crazy dogs just like ours.

* * *

By the end of the lesson Ruckus is doing things I never thought he'd do. He's walking around a pylon, first one way and then the next. He's got his front paws on a small stool and is shuffling his butt around. He looks like a circus dog.

"Let's put him back in the crate," says the trainer, her hands on her hips. She is really good. All business. Ruckus respects her.

I throw a piece of cheese inside his crate, and he dives in. I close the door behind him. He did it. We *all* did. Even Mom got into the ring and made Ruckus sit and pay attention to her.

On the ride home Mom and Hazel talk about the lesson, their voices rising and falling. All I know is that Ruckus is a rock star. That's what the trainer called him. She said dogs like him, who put their whole heart into it, are the best to train.

I look inside the crate. Ruckus is fast asleep, that deep sleep where he lies on his side with all his feet stretched out.

Mom says agility class is every Saturday morning. She says it's going to save our lives. "No more chaos. Thanks to Dad."

"Dad?" I ask.

"It was his idea," says Mom. "And he paid for it."

"He's still going to be in our lives, right?" asks Hazel.

"Of course," says Mom.

"Are you guys staying apart for good?" I ask.

The question just jumps out of my mouth. I don't know why. I guess I've been thinking about it for a long time, and it didn't want to stay inside anymore. I hold my breath, waiting for Mom to answer.

"I think we're happier this way," she says. "Living apart. It took a few months to realize it, but we're sure. We're both really sure."

I let my breath out slowly. "Okay," I say. "I just wanted to know the plan. It was hard not knowing."

"I'm sorry about that," she says, looking at me in the rearview mirror. "I wish I could have known sooner."

"That's okay, Mom," says Hazel.

"One more thing," I say.

Hazel throws me a hard look, but I need to know.

"Would you ever give Ruckus back?" I ask.

"He's not going anywhere," says Mom. "He's stuck with us. We're family, and we take care of each other."

I lean back in my seat. "You hear that?"

Ruckus is snoring. His tail is flipping around his butt like he's dreaming good things. His jaws open and snap shut.

We get to keep our Jack Russell terror.

Acknowledgments

Thank you to the talented and supportive Wildwood Writers: Kari Jones, Julie Paul and Alisa Gordaneer. We have written together for years, taken courses together and critiqued one another's work. Every writer needs a village, and they are mine.

I'd like to acknowledge the support of Liz Kemp at Orca Book Publishers for her editing skills and encouragement. Thank you to my husband, Clay, for his big-hearted love of our crazy dog. And to the dog, thank you for the way you dive into life nose first, tail spinning with excitement.